P9-DWK-813

A Mouse Told His Mother

A Mouse Told His Mother

by Bethany Roberts ★ Illustrated by Maryjane Begin

Little, Brown and Company

Boston   New York   London

First Edition

Library of Congress Cataloging-in-Publication Data
Roberts, Bethany.
     A mouse told his mother / by Bethany Roberts ; illustrated by
Maryjane Begin. — 1st ed.
     p. cm.
     Summary: A little mouse's imagination makes his bedtime an exciting
adventure, as he takes a fantasy trip to catch crocodiles, ride bucking
broncos, and sail where the wind blows.
     ISBN 0-316-74982-6 (hc)   ISBN 0-316-74958-3 (pb)
     [1. Bedtime — Fiction. 2. Imagination — Fiction. 3. Mice — Fiction.]
I. Begin-Callahan, Maryjane, ill. II. Title
PZ7.R5396Mo 1997
[E] — dc20   90-6400

10 9 8 7 6 5 4 3 2

SC

Printed in Hong Kong

*To my parents, who believed
I could be anything I wanted to be
B. R.*

*To "The Boys"—Kit, Chuck, and Craig
M. B.*

A mouse told his mother,
"I am going on a trip."
"It is bedtime," said his mother.

A mouse told his mother,
"I am going to the moon."
"Take your toothbrush," said his mother.

A mouse told his mother,
"I am off to catch a crocodile."
"Don't forget to wash your feet,"
said his mother.

A mouse told his mother,
"I will dive for pirate treasure."
"You'd better bring a towel,"
said his mother.

A mouse told his mother,
"I will climb up snowcapped mountains."
"Wear warm pajamas," said his mother.

A mouse told his mother,
"I will hop into an airplane
and fly around the world."
"Hop right into bed now," said his mother.

A mouse told his mother,
"I will ride a bucking bronco."
"Here's your pillow," said his mother.

A mouse told his mother,
"I'll cross burning desert sands."
"How about a glass of water?"
asked his mother.

A mouse told his mother,
"I'll drive sled dogs through a blizzard."
"You may need an extra blanket,"
said his mother.

A mouse told his mother,
"I'll explore a spooky cave."
"Lights out now," said his mother.

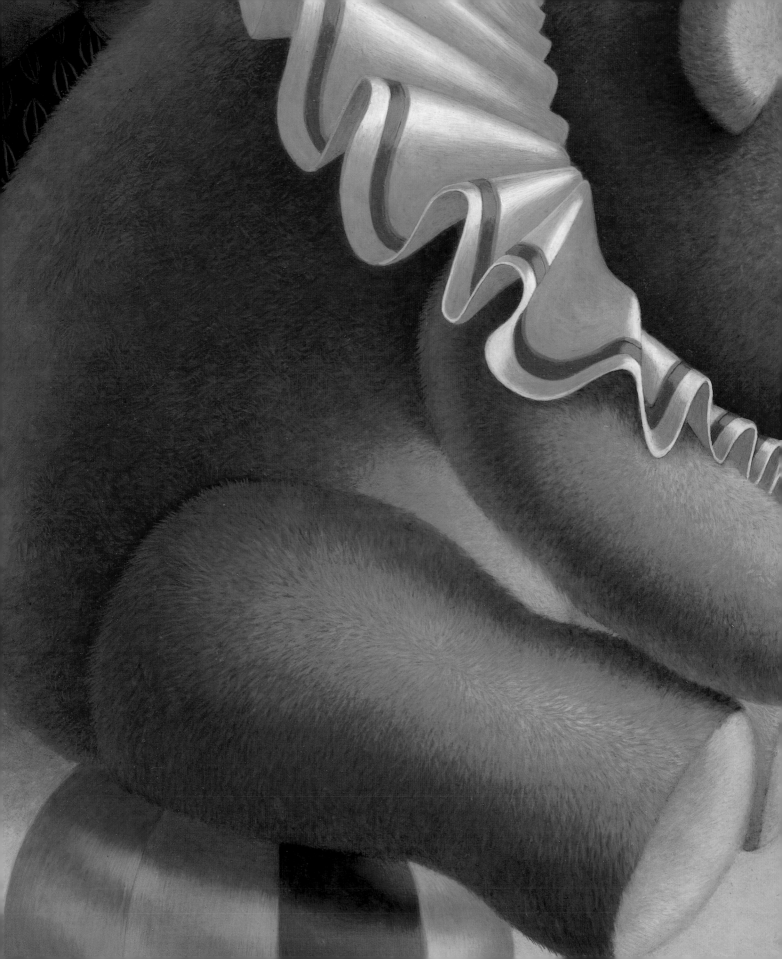

A mouse told his mother,
"I'll tame bears in a circus."
"Here's a bear hug," said his mother.

A mouse told his mother,
"I will sail where the wind blows."
"Blow me a kiss," said his mother.

A mouse told his mother,
"I will come back home again."
"Sweet dreams," said his mother.

"And good night."